The GREAT food BANK HEIST

Onjali Q. Raúf

Illustrated by
Elisa Paganelli

Barrington Stoke

First published in 2021 in Great Britain by
Barrington Stoke Ltd
18 Walker Street, Edinburgh, EH3 7LP

www.barringtonstoke.co.uk

A CIP catalogue record for this book is available
from the British Library upon request

ISBN: 978-1-78112-962-3

Printed by Hussar Books, Poland

*For all tummies fighting daily
battles against hunger.*

*And every s/hero working
tirelessly to end those battles
once and for all.*

For Khalid
With Love &
Light

CONTENTS

1. Just One More Day ...　　　1

2. The Greatest Bank
in the World　　　10

3. Breakfast Club　　　17

4. Games & Empty Bags　　　28

5. The Real Hunger Games　　　36

6. The Last Pawn　　　41

7. Stake-Outs　　　53

8. Supermarket Sweep　　　65

9. The Equaliser　　　78

CHAPTER 1

Just One More Day ...

"Nelson, I'm hungry! I can't wait any more. Look – my tummy's gone in!"

I looked at my sister, Ashley, as she lifted up her T-shirt and sucked her tummy in just as hard as she could. She knew I hated it when she did that, because it looked horrible – as if her tummy was being sucked down a hole.

"All right, all right!" I said, putting down my pen and getting up from the living-room floor. I would have to finish my homework later.

I was hungry too. School dinners never filled me up any more. For some reason, the dinner ladies always gave extra-small helpings on the days when the food was really nice – like fish finger and chips days. And was it just me, or were the fish fingers getting more skinny every week, as if all the fish in the sea were on a diet? Breakfast Club was still OK, but the cereal boxes felt like they were getting smaller too ...

Ashley stomped into the kitchen with me, her ponytail swinging from side to side. She was hugging her favourite toy of the week. This week it was one of my old plastic cars, which she had decided to call Freddy. No one knew why.

She jumped up onto her favourite chair at the kitchen table, patted Freddy and then looked at me hopefully.

It was time again.

Time for me to play the Pretend Game.

The Pretend Game was when I had to pretend we had food left in the house even when we didn't.

I hated playing the Pretend Game. Out of all the games I had to play at home, it was the worst one. Especially when it was coming to the end of what Mum called "A Really Tricky Month". That's a month where the money Mum got from her job wasn't enough to pay for food as well as everything else we needed. But this month we were lucky. Someone had given Mum some vouchers, and I knew that tomorrow we would be heading down to the best Bank in the world to cash one of them in.

"Hmm," I said as I went over to the fridge and opened the door wide.

The fridge lit up with a warm yellow glow, as if it wanted to show us that it had something inside for us to eat. But the shelves were empty apart from half a jar of jam, a plastic bottle of mustard that had been there since before I was born, one egg and a tiny bit of milk.

I could have boiled the egg for Ashley, but I knew Mum probably hadn't eaten all day at work, so I wanted to save it for her.

"Nope, nothing interesting in there," I said, closing the fridge door. "Let's try here!"

In the cupboard next to the fridge there were packets of spices and salt someone at the Bank had once given us but which we had never used, a bottle of oil and half a packet of cornflakes. I could have given Ashley cornflakes, but I needed to save the milk for when Mum came home and wanted a cup of tea.

I shut the door, then opened the next one, and the next one, and the next one. And the whole time I pretended there might be something inside to eat – even though I could have told Ashley what was in every single cupboard with my eyes closed.

I wished they were filled with food like my best friends Krish and Harriet's cupboards always were. When I grew up, I was definitely going to have cupboards like they had.

"We have to wait for Mum to get back," I said to Ashley. "She'll be here soon. Maybe she'll have picked something up on the way home."

"But I'm really, really, reeeeeeeally hungry," said Ashley, lifting up her T-shirt and getting ready to suck in her tummy again.

But before she could do it, I grabbed the toy car and ran off with it.

"FREDDY!" Ashley shouted, and ran after me. I didn't really want to play, but I knew if I kept Ashley busy, she'd forget she was hungry. At least for a few minutes.

As I held Freddy high in the air and watched Ashley jump up and down like a human rabbit to try to grab it, we heard the sound of keys in the door. Mum was back!

"Kids?"

"Mummy!" squealed Ashley. She forgot about Freddy, ran to Mum and hugged her tight.

Mum smiled as I poked my head out of the living-room door. I only looked after Ashley for half an hour every day when we got home from school, but it always felt like ages.

"All right, all right, my little hugging machine," laughed Mum as she gave Ashley a kiss on the top of her head. I could tell Mum was tired, because her eyes were puffy. That meant she had had to work extra hard.

Mum worked as a nurse in a hospital, looking after lots of sick people who had just had serious operations. She had to take their temperatures and measure their heartbeats and make sure they had taken their medicines on time.

"Mum, I'm HUNGRY and Nelson hasn't given me or Freddy ANYTHING to eat," reported Ashley.

Mum looked over at me and gave her sad smile. I hated that smile. That was the other thing I wished for – even more than I wished for all the kitchen cupboards to be full. I wished I would never have to see Mum's sad smile ever again. The one that tried to hide how bad she felt about us not having enough to eat – even when she worked so hard and hardly ate anything herself.

"Well, come on then, let's see what magic we can find," said Mum. She gave me a pat on the cheek and hugged Ashley as we walked into the kitchen.

After looking through the cupboards just like I had done a few minutes ago, Mum shook her head.

"Just one more day," she promised as she took out the egg, the tiny bit of milk, the jam and a tin of kidney beans that was right at the back of the bottom cupboard. "Then we can go to the Bank and get the things we need. But for now it's time to do a bit of magic with the things we have ..."

As we all sat down to a dinner of a tiny omelette, a bowl of heated kidney beans and a

dessert of cornflakes dipped in jam, I felt my
stomach swirl and growl. I crossed my arms on
top of it to stop it from making any more noises
and whispered to myself the thing that Mum
had just said.

"Just one more day," I said as softly as I
could. "And then you can have everything
you need ..."

CHAPTER 2

The Greatest Bank in the World

The next morning I woke up extra early and jumped out of bed.

Whenever it was a Voucher Thursday, Mum always finished her shift early and picked me and Ashley up from school so we could go straight to the Bank with lots of carrier bags stuffed into our pockets.

Our Bank – the one we always went to at the end of a Really Tricky Month – was *the* best, *the* most fun and *the* greatest bank in the world.

That's because our Bank wasn't anything like any of the boring old money banks you see on the high street, which are always grey and have big machines which swallow up cards and spit out bits of paper at you, and which are filled with grey-looking people who are always bending over notes and coins.

Our Bank – the food bank – was full of people in bright clothes who always smiled and asked us how we were doing. They were so kind and funny that they even made Mum forget about being embarrassed and ashamed about having to go to the Bank to get us food. Mrs Patel and Mr Anthony and a girl called Natasha – who had hair as thick as a horse's tail! – were my favourite bankers. We'd known them for nearly a whole year. Ever since Dad left us to go and make a new family that he wanted to be with more than us.

I wished every bank near us was like the food bank. No other bank in the world had

shining tins and rustling packets of delicious food stacked from the floor to the roof. No other bank let you take things out without you putting money into it first. And no other bank had a sign by the front counter that said: "Money Not Welcome Here". It was the only place in the world, I think, that didn't like money. I wished the man who owned our flat and took rent money from Mum was like our Bank. He was always asking for more money – he never had enough to make him happy.

I picked up my school rucksack, took out my Homework Diary and flipped it to the back page. There, in extra-light pencil so that no one would see, was my Bank Withdrooling List.

My Bank Withdrooling List was a list of every single thing I had ever wanted to withdraw from the Bank and bring home for us to eat. You know, things that make your mouth go all watery and your tummy start to lick its lips and drool too!

This was what I had on my list so far:

BANK WITHDROOLING LIST

1. Choco-loco Nutty Melts

2. Chocolate spread

3. Cheese and onion crisps

4. Fizzy cola pop

5. Pizzas

6. Fish fingers

7. Frozen chips

8. Chocolate biscuits

9. Things to make in the microwave so I don't have to cook

10. Jam swiss roll (for Mum)

11. Butter (real butter, not the fake stuff in a tub)

12. Something green like peas so we can be healthy

13. Emergency pasta for when we run out of stuff

14. Kinder Eggs

When it was a Really Tricky Month and I got so hungry that I thought I might fade away, I loved looking at my list and dreaming that I had all of those things to eat right away.

Nobody knew about my list. Not even Mum, or Krish or Harriet – even though they were my best friends. It was embarrassing making lists about food you wished you could eat when everyone else was making lists about computer games and toys that they wanted for their birthdays and Christmas and Eid and Diwali and other special days.

It was my Golden Goal to bring all the things on my list home from the Bank one day.

It hadn't happened because normally the food the Bank gave us was serious – like bread and baked beans and potatoes and Weetabix. There weren't any fun things like chocolate biscuits or crisps. But Mrs Patel always gave me and Ashley some treats as well, so for at least the week after a visit, we knew we'd have some chocolate.

Getting out a pencil, I closed my eyes and imagined what I would be eating right now if I could. The picture my mind came up with made my stomach drool extra hard. So I wrote it down:

15. Chocolate muffins

Then I snapped my Homework Diary shut and got ready for school just as quickly as I could. I was never, ever late for Breakfast Club, and today I wanted to be the first one there.

CHAPTER 3

Breakfast Club

There was one rule to being a member of Breakfast Club and that was you never talked about Breakfast Club. At least, not with anyone who didn't go to Breakfast Club.

Our Breakfast Club at school was one of the best because Mrs Bell and Mr Ramjit ran it. Mrs Bell was our head teacher and Mr Ramjit was her deputy.

Mrs Bell was always super strict about Breakfast Club. Everyone had to get there by 8 a.m. and be sitting down by exactly 8.05 a.m., and everyone had to choose a piece of fruit, a drink, and have one bowl of cereal and a piece of toast with one spread on it.

I always chose a banana for my fruit if there were any left, any cereal that had chocolate in it, and chocolate spread or jam to go on my toast. Sometimes I wished I could have four pieces of toast and not just one. Especially on a Monday when we hadn't had enough to eat at the weekend.

On Fridays at Breakfast Club, everyone got a treat! Nobody ever knew what the treat was going to be because Mrs Bell bought it the night before with her very own money. The best treat was donuts or cookies. The worst was cold pots of yoghurt! But none of us really minded. The most exciting thing was trying to guess what it might be.

I always tried to get to Breakfast Club super early because I didn't want Krish and Harriet to see me going into the hall for it. They were lucky and had lots of food at home, so they didn't need to go to Breakfast Club.

Krish and Harriet were my two best friends. We did everything together – except Breakfast Club.

Krish was the shortest – and skinniest – boy in our whole year. He wanted to be a spy when he grew up. I thought he would be good at it because he was so skinny that he could hide behind a lamp post if he needed to and the bad guys would never see him!

It was funny Krish was so skinny, because he never stopped eating. His pockets were always full of sweets and mints and football stickers, and he always had the best haircuts because he copied the styles of our favourite footballers.

Right now, our favourite footballer was Noah Equiano – the whole world called him The Equaliser because he always levelled any game he played in before he scored the winning goal. And the best thing about him was that he was born in our town and had gone to a school only twenty minutes away! Me and Krish kept telling our parents to transfer us to that other school, but they said we didn't need to go to the same school as Noah Equiano to be as good at football as him. Parents don't know anything sometimes.

Harriet wasn't into football as much as me and Krish. She loved car racing and was always talking about circuits and lap times and horse-powers. She liked Equiano, but only because he came from our town. She thought Desiree Chadwick was much better because she was the first woman to win a Formula One Grand Prix in over forty years. Harriet loved arguing with us and wanted to be an inventor when she grew up. She was extra super-clever, so both me and Krish thought she could definitely become one.

I wished Krish and Harriet didn't know that I was hungry a lot of the time, but they did. We never talked about it, but they still knew. And I wished I could play with them in the mornings instead of having to go to Breakfast Club, but I needed Breakfast Club to get the energy, so I pretended I didn't come to school until later and I never told them about it.

"Morning, Nelson," said Mr Ramjit as I walked into the hall.

"Morning, sir." I grinned as I walked past him and grabbed the first banana I saw.

"Your favourite's in today," said Mrs Bell, giving me a nod. "Chocolate hoops," she whispered as I grabbed a box. It wasn't every day we had chocolate hoops! I was so hungry I could have eaten ten boxes, but I didn't try to sneak another one and just went quickly over to Maureen, the dinner lady, to get myself some toast.

"What'll it be this morning, Nelson?" she asked, holding a knife between the chocolate spread jar and the jam jar.

It was an important question, so I took a moment to work out what my stomach really wanted. It growled loudest at the thought of chocolate spread, so I chose that.

"Good lad," said Maureen, nodding so hard it made her curly grey hairs look like they were having a disco but nobody else could hear the music.

I sat down in the spot I liked best, which was at the back of the hall. I ate the banana as quickly as I could and then reached out for the milk jug in the middle of the table.

"Hey, Nelson!"

"Hey, Lavinia!"

Lavinia came and sat next to me. She had bright orange hair that always looked as if it had been electrocuted.

Lavinia didn't say anything else. She chewed on her food slowly and gave a loud gulp every seven seconds, then looked over at everyone in Breakfast Club like a giant, human owl.

"Hey, Nelson, what do you think Mrs Bell's gonna get us tomorrow?" asked Leon as he gave a silent nod to Lavinia and then filled his mouth with an enormous bite of apple.

I shrugged. "Chocolate muffins?" I said hopefully.

"They're way too expensive!" said William as he sat down next to us. He made sure Mrs Bell wasn't looking, then licked the jam on his toast with the tip of his tongue, just like a lizard.

"Those things are like a pound for each one," William carried on. "She can't afford that! Dad says teachers get paid bupkis. I don't know what a bupkis is, but I know it's not a lot, so Mrs Bell definitely can't afford chocolate muffins for all of us!"

No one said anything else. We all ate our breakfasts and watched as more members of the club came into the hall.

"Hey, you guys, did you hear that there's something wrong with the food bank?"

We all looked up at Kerry as she slammed down her tray and flicked back her long brown hair. Kerry was always late and loved talking loudly. She was in Ms Potter's class two doors down from mine, and we could still always hear her.

"No," I said. "Why? What's wrong with the food bank?"

"I dunno. But Mum and Dad went last night, and Kwan's gran went the night before that, and it looks like they don't have as much food there as usual."

Kerry sat down and added, "Kwan's gran said the bankers think someone's stealing stuff, but they don't know who!"

"Whoah!" said William as he started to lick at his cereal with his lizard tongue. "Why would anyone steal stuff from a food bank?"

"Yeah," said Leon, gulping down his apple. "Especially when there's a real bank with actual money in it right next door!"

Kerry gave a shrug. "Cos they must be really thick, I guess. Mum says it's not right – it's not fair."

William shook his head. "We're lucky it's not happening at Breakfast Club too, then. Isn't it?"

We all stopped chewing and turned our heads to where Maureen, the dinner lady, was standing and looked at the big table of fruit and cereals next to her. It didn't look as if anyone would dare to steal stuff from her.

"It better not happen here," said Leon, chewing his apple extra fast.

"Yeah. Well, just in case, you better all eat as much as you can at lunch-time – because who knows?" Kerry warned as Mrs Bell gave a loud clap to tell us that we only had a few minutes left.

Right away everyone stopped talking and the noisy hall fell quiet. All you could hear was loud slurps and spoons banging on the bottom of bowls.

I ate my toast as quickly as I could. What if the Bank didn't have enough food for Mum and me and Ashley tonight? I put my arms over my tummy again as it gave an extra-loud and worried growl ...

CHAPTER 4

Games & Empty Bags

I was still worrying about the food bank when the bell rang for the end of school.

"Your mum's here!" shouted Krish, waving at my mum like she had come to pick him up instead.

"Awesome," I said with a grin as I saw Ashley speed towards the school gates. She was still hugging Freddy as if it was a teddy bear.

Krish and Harriet joined me as I headed towards the gates too.

"What game will you play with your mum today?" asked Harriet, giving me a nudge on my elbow with her elbow.

I looked over at her and grinned. "Mum's always coming up with new ones, so I don't know."

"Wish my mum would come up with fun games to play," said Krish. "But she thinks I-Spy is hilarious, so that's the only game we ever get to play with her."

"Nelson's mum's the coolest," nodded Harriet as she sucked in her lips and made an opening and closing fish mouth. It was her favourite thing to do, and she did it so much I don't think she even knew she was doing it most of the time.

"Yeah, guess," I said, doing my best not to grin. Mum really was the coolest.

"Hi, Krish, hi, Harriet," said Mum as she smiled at us.

Krish's light brown cheeks suddenly flushed so bright red it was like watching a traffic light change colour.

Harriet covered a snigger with her hand before saying, "Hi, Ms James."

"Hi," blurted out Krish.

"Nice to see you both looking so well," said Mum. "Krish, you must have grown ... let's see, at least three millimetres since last week!"

"You really think so?" asked Krish, trying to stand as straight and as tall as he could.

"Why don't you both come over on Sunday?" asked Mum. "It'll be nice for Nelson to have you at ours for once, instead of me dropping him and Ashley over at your houses all the time."

"Yeah! And can you bring lots of snacks too?" asked Ashley. "And then leave them? I like prawn cocktail crisps the best! And chocolate Penguins – even though they're not really penguins."

Now it was Mum's and my turn to turn into traffic lights, because I knew both our faces went red at the exact same time.

"Oh, don't you worry about that," said Mum. "I'll sort out some snacks!"

"Nah, Ms James, I eat TONNES!" said Krish. "I love bringing stuff to yours. Mum always gives me stuff that she only lets me have for treats when you invite us round."

"Yeah, and we've got WAY too many prawn cocktail crisps at home," added Harriet. "Nobody eats them – they're like the worst ones!"

I looked at Harriet and didn't know what to say, because I had seen her eat three packets of prawn cocktail crisps in one go and then lick the inside of the packets too!

"Ah – well, if you must," smiled Mum, giving my hand a secret squeeze. She was trying to make me feel better.

"Right, then, we better be off," said Mum. She took Ashley's hand and waved at Harriet and Krish. "Give your parents my love!"

Krish and Harriet waved back as they turned to go home too.

"So, what game shall we play today?" asked Mum as we began the forty-minute walk to the Bank. We could have got the bus, but Mum only let us do that if it was raining, because she needed to save as much travel money as she could.

On this walk, Mum decided to play the Animal Spirit game with us, where we had to look at the people walking past and imagine what animal spirits they might be. Ashley pointed at anyone wearing something glittery and shiny and announced they were a unicorn, but I spotted someone who could easily have been a crocodile, and another person who was definitely a human bumble bee – mainly because he was wearing a yellow and black striped jumper.

When we got to the Bank and had to wait for our turn, Mum played the Guessing Game with us. That was when Ashley had to guess what food we might get to take home that day. Mostly she got it wrong because she was only six and only cared about chocolate biscuits and sweets. But it was still fun to play.

And then, when Mum was sorting out our vouchers with Mrs Patel and Mr Anthony, and Natasha was getting us our things, me and Ashley played the Keeping Time game. That was when we tried to guess what Natasha was getting for us by how long it took her to go and get each thing.

"Right, kids ... Looks like there's a bit of a problem," said Mum as she came back from the counter with just two bags and not the four or five we got every other time.

"Do we have to wait longer?" I asked as I took a bag from Mum and looked inside. There was a loaf of brown bread that Ashley didn't like, a packet of rolls and two tins of baked beans instead of the normal four.

"Seems the Bank is a little short this month," said Mum, taking a deep breath. "But that's OK. We can make do, can't we, my little troopers?"

Ashley didn't say anything, and I gave a silent nod. When Mum said "little troopers", we both knew it was going to be a hard month ahead. Even harder than normal ...

Then I remembered what Kerry had told us at Breakfast Club about someone stealing food from the Bank!

As I watched Mum trying to pretend that everything was fine, I promised myself that I would find out what was going on. And make it stop.

CHAPTER 5

The Real Hunger Games

I hated the months when we had to be little troopers. They were always hard because the games we played at home suddenly didn't feel like fun any more. Nothing was ever fun when you were so hungry you felt as if you were full of gaps and holes.

Normally the games we played made everything feel ten thousand per cent better. And that was all because of Mum. She became a games inventor when Dad left us and she had to go to the food bank for the first time. She came home with some things we liked and lots we didn't like at all. So to stop me and Ashley feeling as if we didn't want to eat the meals she made, Mum came up with all sorts of games.

My favourite one had to be Master Chef, which was when I got to choose all the weirdest ingredients the food bank had given us and cook a meal out of them. Mum's friend from the hospital had even given me a real chef's hat with a real burnt hole in it to wear when I was playing it!

So far I'd come up with gherkin hot dogs, tuna and jam pie, and noodles swirled with mustard and brown sauce. But the dish I was most famous for was Pineapple Surprise, which was bread soaked in lemonade and fried, topped with large, round pineapple slices from a tin and put in the oven so that it looked like a burger. I'd never seen Mum's face look so funny as when she was eating that one!

The game Ashley loved best was the Menu Makers Game. We played that after every visit to the Bank. We made a list of everything the food bank had given us and then invented a proper menu – just like you get in a restaurant.

Ashley loved drawing and colouring in, so her menus were always the prettiest. When she did an extra-special one, Mum stuck it on the fridge. My favourite menu Ashley made was covered with pictures of mushrooms with salad leaves as wings, and fish with lots of fingers.

But there was one game we didn't really enjoy at all. Even Mum didn't like it, although she pretended she did. It was called the Transformers Game. We always played that in a Little Troopers Month, and sometimes we had to play it a few times.

It was where you looked at food that you didn't want to eat – not even a little bit! – and used your imagination to make it into something extra tasty and delicious, and then told everyone about it. Mum said she had invented it to help our imaginations grow stronger.

It was hard, but sometimes it did work. One time I transformed a horrible, lumpy, bright red sandwich filled with nothing but extra-squashy wet tomatoes into a huge roast chicken with a mountain of mashed potatoes with lots of butter melting down it like a volcano. I didn't have those things, but imagining them made me not mind eating the sandwich so much.

But in a Little Troopers Month, playing any of those games felt like hard work.

It was hard trying to make a menu when you didn't have much food to write out on it. And it was hard being a Master Chef when there weren't enough ingredients, no matter how nice and burnt-looking the hole in your chef's hat was. And it was especially hard when you had spent a whole day thinking about food – even in the middle of playing football or reading a book or trying to figure out your nine times table – and made yourself tired. At times like that your imagination sometimes didn't want to transform something horrible into something better.

And sometimes none of the games worked at all, and everyone was just acting and pretending that they weren't hungry when really they were so hungry that they couldn't sleep at night and cried when they thought no one else could hear them ... Even Mum ... Especially Mum.

CHAPTER 6

The Last Pawn

At Breakfast Club that week, and the week after that, all anyone could talk about was the food bank and the fact that it didn't seem to have much food any more.

Leon said the thieves had taken so many things that the Bank would need to shut down soon. But then William said that would be illegal and that the army would come to help and give us the sugar and tea and butter that we needed, just like they did in World War Two. Kerry said that it didn't matter as long as we still had Breakfast Club and free dinners at school – except that maybe we would need to wear clothes with more pockets so we could save things to take home.

But as more weeks went by, things got worse. Mrs Bell saw that we weren't talking or playing as much as we normally did, so she began to give out extra portions of fruit and toast. But it still wasn't enough. Nothing was big enough to fill the giant black holes in our tummies. Even Lavinia's red hair had started looking less electrocuted.

Krish and Harriet could see that I was feeling tired all the time, so they tried to give me food by pretending that they suddenly didn't like their favourite things any more or had eaten too much already. I knew they were lying, so one day I told them to just stop it and to leave me alone.

"Stop what?" asked Harriet, looking shocked, while Krish stared at me with a cereal bar hanging out of his mouth.

"Just stop feeling sorry for me! I'm fine!" I shouted, feeling red-hot angry. "I don't want your stupid biscuit!"

"I only asked if you wanted to share it with me!" said Harriet, getting angry too. I could tell because her nostrils were moving up and down.

Krish was frowning and staring at me too as the cereal bar in his mouth began to crumble. Suddenly, I felt stupid as my stomach gave a roar so loud that everyone could hear.

"Sorry ..." I said. "It's just ..."

Krish slowly took a step towards me, as if I was a crocodile who might bite his head off.

"Did we do something wrong?" he asked.

I gave up. I knew I had to tell them, because if everyone at Breakfast Club was right, then me and Mum and Ashley were going to starve soon. In fact, we were already starving. This month felt harder than the last one. Last night we only had half a slice of toast each for dinner and Ashley had fallen asleep crying. Her insides were beginning to hurt again.

So I broke the Breakfast Club rule and told Harriet and Krish what everyone was saying about our Bank being robbed.

"That's horrible!" cried Krish.

"Why would anyone steal anything from a food bank?" asked Harriet. She stopped being angry with me and got angry with the thieves instead.

I shrugged. "Don't know. But it means everyone just feels hungry all the time."

"Maybe the thieves are *selling* all the stuff they're stealing from the food bank," muttered Harriet. She shoved the chocolate biscuit into my hand, and I gobbled it down as she carried on talking.

"But ... how are they taking everything? Are they breaking into the Bank every night?" she asked.

I shook my head. The bankers had told everyone that no one had broken into the warehouse at all.

"Wait. Where does all the food for the Bank come from again?" asked Krish.

"From people at the supermarkets," I said. "They donate things and put them in a special trolley, and then the supermarkets take everything to the Bank. And then the bankers put the food on the shelves and give it to us."

"Cool," said Krish.

"Well, if it's not being nicked straight from the Bank, then the thieves have *got* to be stealing things from the supermarkets," said Harriet. "Mum and Dad always give our donations to Gladstores – the big one up the road. We buy extra stuff and put it in the food bank trolleys just like you said."

"Gladstores is the one that gives my Bank all its food!" I said. I suddenly felt embarrassed – what if I had been eating food that Harriet and her mum and dad gave away to the food bank? Now I knew why Mum didn't like taking things from a charity. It was embarrassing to have to eat things that your friends had donated ...

"Hey, maybe we should do a stake-out at Gladstores!" said Krish, getting excited.

"You mean a stake-out when you go and spy on people?" I asked.

"Yeah," answered Krish. "We could go under cover after school and find out how the robbers are stealing the food. If we catch them and take them to the police, maybe we could get a special medal too!"

"But how would we do a stake-out at Gladstores?" I asked. "It's HUGE! The thieves would be mad to steal things with loads of people about."

"And don't they have a million cameras and security guards and things?" asked Harriet. "They'd have caught the thieves by now, wouldn't they?"

"Maybe," said Krish. He scratched his head
and gave us a shrug as we all thought about
what else we could do.

*

We soon forgot all about Krish's stake-out idea,
but then something happened which made me
so angry that I knew we had to do something.

The following weeks were good weeks
because Mum got paid and could buy enough
food with her own money to stop our stomachs
from growling all the time. We were down to
our last food bank voucher, and I knew Mum
wasn't going to use it until she had to.

But then she did have to because the greedy
rent man sent a letter telling us that Mum had
to pay more rent or leave. After she had paid
him, Mum had to take us to the Bank again
right away. But when we got there, Mrs Patel
and Mr Anthony and Natasha could only give us

one and a half bags of food. They all said sorry a hundred times and looked so sad that it made me start to feel scared.

And then, the next week, Mum came home with the hugest bags of shopping me and Ashley had ever seen. They were filled with treats and packets of all the delicious things we loved but hadn't eaten in a long time.

There were chicken nuggets for Ashley, burgers for me and chips for us all, and Mum's favourite dessert – jam swiss roll!

It was as if Christmas had come, except there wasn't a man with a giant belly trying to come down a chimney we didn't have!

As Ashley skipped around the kitchen singing, Mum turned on the oven and put in two burgers – one each for me and her – seven chicken nuggets for Ashley, and exactly thirty-three chips. I looked at Mum and frowned. Something was different.

"Mum, where did you get so much money from all of a sudden?" I asked as I helped set the table for what was going to be the best meal we had had in ages. I knew her payday wasn't for at least another week.

"Oh ... just a bit of luck!" said Mum, giving me a wink.

And then suddenly I noticed it – the thing that was different ...

It was the empty space on her finger.

"Mum!" I cried out. "Nan's ring ..."

Heading over to the fridge, Mum opened the door and pretended she was looking for something inside it. My insides were getting too heavy, so I went and opened a cupboard door and put my head inside that.

We always ended up like that whenever I found out that Mum had paid a visit to the pawn shop.

When I was little, I used to think pawn shops had made a spelling mistake and that they sold prawns but had just forgotten to put the "r" in. But they hadn't, because they don't really sell anything at all. Not even prawns.

They let you borrow money in exchange for your most precious, most expensive things. And then, if you ever earn enough money again, you

can go and buy your things back from them.
But that never happens. Not for Mum anyway.

As I sat with my head in the cupboard, I
made a promise that when I grew up, I would
get a job that paid me millions of pounds and I
would go and buy back Nan's ring just as quick
as I could!

But for now, I wouldn't let Mum take any
more of her things to the pawn shop. Nan's ring
had to be the last pawn – ever! So as I waited
for Mum to leave the fridge, I decided Krish was
right. It was time to make a stake-out plan and
catch the food bank thieves.

CHAPTER 7
Stake-Outs

The next morning at school, I told Krish he had been right and that we needed to do a stake-out.

"You mean it? Really?" asked Krish. He gave me a happy punch on the arm and started jumping up and down on the spot too.

"Let's do it today! After school," said Harriet, pulling us all together so no one could hear what we were saying. "We could run down to Gladstores – it's only a few minutes away!"

"But I've got Ashley, remember?" I reminded her. "AND I need to be home before Mum gets in."

"You can just come for a short while then," answered Harriet. "And me and Krish can stay a little bit longer! Yeah?"

Krish nodded, and so did I. So right after school, we all ran to Gladstores. I told Ashley we were playing a special game and that if she was good, she could have something I had saved for her from my school dinner as a treat.

When we got to the supermarket, we tried to secretly spy on the food bank trolleys by walking up and down the aisles and watching the people who put things in the trolleys. But we didn't see anything weird going on.

We did the same thing the next day, and the next, and the next. But all we saw were lots of people putting things *into* the food bank trolleys.

"This isn't working," said Krish, after we had been to the supermarket every day after school for nearly two weeks. By now the security

guard was beginning to give us strange looks –
he probably thought *we* were trying to steal
something. "Maybe the thieves have got kids, so
they don't do any robbing after they've picked
them up from school?"

"Maybe," said Harriet. "What we really need is a whole day to try and catch them ... I know! Why don't we try this Saturday?"

"Yeah," I cried. "Mum has to work on Saturday, so she'll be dropping me and Ashley off at yours anyway."

"Yeah, I know," answered Harriet, looking at me as if I was stupid. "That's why I said Saturday in the first place!"

"Cool," I replied.

"And that gives us a few days to plan and train hard so we can be super-fast and sneaky and strong," added Krish. "I know all about that stuff, so I'll train you both. Deal?"

I nodded and so did Harriet. But then she added, "But I'll do the planning! So you have to listen to me about that. OK?"

Krish and me nodded, and over the next few days we planned our big stake-out and did lots of training. Harriet drew out a plan on four pieces of paper stuck together with tape, and Krish trained us at break-times and lunch-times so we'd be extra fit and strong.

The training was mostly zig-zag running through the playground at top speed, just like Noah Equiano did on the football pitch, and doing karate chops and flying kicks, even in the middle of class. Everyone thought we were weird, but it was fun, so we didn't care.

By Friday night, we were ready.

On Saturday morning, after Mum had kissed me and Ashley goodbye, Harriet's mum took us upstairs to Harriet's room. Krish was already there, playing a computer game with Harriet as they waited for us – along with a mini mountain of food. That was the best thing about Harriet's house. There were always mini mountains of food everywhere.

As soon as Harriet's mum had shut the bedroom door behind her and we heard her head back downstairs, we all set to work.

I quickly packed all the food into mine and Ashley's rucksacks. Harriet got four tubs of bright green and purple slime from under her bed and packed them into hers. She also switched on her speaker so that, together with her computer game, everything in her room sounded noisy and busy. Then she sneaked downstairs to get our coats. She made it back without being seen and helped me zip up Ashley's coat and explain to her that we were going on an extra-special secret adventure.

Krish had disappeared to the bathroom and suddenly came back into the room wearing a Spiderman ski mask and carrying something red and sticky and wrapped in plastic in both his hands.

Everyone stopped what they were doing and stared at Krish with their mouths open. Even Ashley.

"Erm … why have you brought ACTUAL steaks to a stake-out?" asked Harriet, her nose all scrunched up.

"D'uh! There might be dogs," said Krish as he squeezed the two steaks into the back pockets of his jeans. "This will distract them. I got them from the shop next door to my house. But I can't touch them or anything because I'm Hindu and Mum and Dad will have a fit. It's disgusting even holding them! Eugh!"

Harriet turned to look at me with her mouth still open, but I understood Krish's point. "He might be right about the dogs," I said. "It's all right, Krish, I'll unwrap them and throw them for you."

Krish nodded, looking as happy as a Hindu vegetarian with meat in his pockets could.

"Anyway, why have *you* got a MASSIVE box of donuts and a flask?" asked Krish, pointing at the box of twelve donuts and the Thermos flask Harriet was holding.

"Because that's what you have to eat on a stake-out – donuts and coffee. That's what they do in ALL the movies," she replied.

I grinned. When Harriet wasn't watching Formula One, she was always watching cop dramas. Especially American ones. That might be why she had stolen her older sister's long brown coat that was too big for her, and a big hat. She was clearly trying to look like the detective from her favourite TV show.

"Got the plan?" I asked Harriet. I was starting to feel nervous.

Harriet nodded and took it out of her coat pocket.

We all looked down at it again. Harriet had drawn in all the different aisles and where the food bank donation trolleys were. And, of course, where the security guard always stood.

Then, in glittery green, purple and blue pen, she had drawn big fat arrows to show what we were all supposed to do.

"Here, take the whistles," Harriet ordered as she gave me and Krish a silver whistle each. "I've wiped them super clean," she added. "Mum's always leaving them all over the house."

Harriet's mum was a football coach, so she had at least five hundred whistles that she was always losing. She even kept some in her socks because she said that was the best place for a spare one.

"OK. Ready?" asked Krish. His voice sounded odd because of the Spiderman mask.

We all nodded to each other and then looked down at Ashley.

"Remember, it's a secret, Ashley. We're going on a secret adventure, so you have to listen to me. OK?" I asked her. But she was so excited that Harriet was letting her take her hand that she didn't really listen to anything I was saying.

Sneaking out of Harriet's room, we all crept down the stairs and towards the front door. Harriet's dad was at his restaurant, so we didn't need to worry about him, but her mum and big sister were downstairs in the living room. Luckily they were talking loudly on their phones and watching TV too.

"Quick!" hissed Harriet as she opened the door and rushed us all out. She closed it again very slowly so that only a small "click" could be heard. Then, waving to us all to copy her and crouch down, we ran past the living-room window and out through the front gate.

"Phew!" said Krish as we got to the end of the road and stood up straight again. "That was easy."

"Again, again!" cried Ashley. She thought it was all a big game we were playing for fun.

"Later," I promised as we began to walk faster and faster towards Gladstores.

Gladstores was only a short walk away, but we felt nervous suddenly, and hungry too, so we each had a donut for luck and then tried the coffee. It was horrible!

As the sign for Gladstores got closer and closer, I could tell Krish and Harriet were asking the same questions in their heads as I was. Questions like: were we ever really going to catch anyone – what if they were too clever for us? What if Harriet's mum or sister went up to Harriet's room and found us all gone? What if we didn't catch anyone at all and got into trouble anyway?

Then, suddenly, we were at the giant sliding doors of the supermarket and the huge sign that said "WELCOME".

It was time for us to split up and try to catch a thief ...

CHAPTER 8
Supermarket Sweep

Harriet went inside first. She gave us a thumbs up and a nervous smile and marched straight up the fruit aisle in her long coat and big hat. Her job was to watch the back exit doors, the ones with the long pieces of plastic on them that the supermarket workers always vanished behind.

Next it was Krish's turn. He waited until two people with a trolley walked past us, and then he walked after them as if he was part of their family. His job was to walk up and down the different aisles and see if he could spot anything fishy. Apart from actual fish, of course.

Then it was my turn.

I took Ashley's hand and went inside, heading straight for the magazine racks. From there I could keep a close watch on the food bank donation trolleys, which were always parked in between the newspaper stand and the red post office box right by the front door. Hanging from the ceiling was a bright green sign that said: "FOOD BANK DONATIONS".

I gave Ashley a comic about turtles to flick through and made her sit on the floor so that it looked as if we were waiting for our mum or dad. I watched the donation trolleys. There were three. One was very full, one was only half full, and the last one was almost empty.

I watched and watched and watched the trolleys as lots of people dropped things into them on their way out. Most put in all the normal things, like boxes of cereals and tins of tomatoes and packets of pasta. But some people put strange things in too: like an old man who put in five packets of chewing gum and a bunch of flowers. And a woman who put in seven packets of red chillies and a basil plant.

"I don't want to read any more," said Ashley, hugging Freddy and standing up. "I want to go back to Harriet's house and play!"

"If you read something else, I'll give you some crisps," I offered as I took a bright pink packet of prawn cocktail flavour crisps from my rucksack and held them out to her.

Ashley nodded and sat back down. As she crunched and gobbled, I gave her another comic to look through and went back to watching the trolleys.

And just as I was beginning to think that no one was stealing from the food bank at all, I saw it happen! The sneakiest of sneak attacks ever!

A man and a woman had stopped by the newspaper stand, pushing a trolley with just two packets of biscuits and a bottle of water in it. They looked as if they were choosing a newspaper to buy, but then suddenly they were gone! They had switched their nearly empty trolley with the food bank trolley full of donations and now they were on their way out of the store with it as if it was theirs!

I blinked hard to check my eyes had seen right and then looked over at the security guard station – but there was no one there! The thieves must have seen that too! So I did the next best thing: I blew on my whistle just as hard as I could and pointed at the couple, shouting, "STOP! FOOD BANK THIEVES!"

The man and the woman looked back at me for a split second and then began to run out of the store. From somewhere behind me, I could hear Harriet and Krish blowing their whistles too, which meant they had heard me and were on their way – but they were going to be too late!

I snatched a trolley that was standing next to me – I didn't care that it had some tins and boxes in it. Then I swooped up Ashley and her rucksack, plonked them into it and ran after the thieves.

As I zigged and zagged and zoomed the trolley past lots of other trolleys, Ashley clapped

her hands and giggled. But just as I pushed us out of the main exit doors, the alarms began to sound! My trolley of unpaid food had set everything off!

"WHEEEEEEEE-WHEEEEEEEEE!" cried Ashley even louder as I sprinted out into the car park.

From somewhere behind me, someone shouted, "OI! YOU KIDS THERE! STOP!"

I ran even faster, trying to see where the man and woman had gone – but there were so many people and too many cars …

A few seconds later, Harriet and Krish came crashing into me.

"Where … where … what …?" asked Krish.

"Trolley switchers!" I tried to explain. "They – they switched a nearly empty trolley for one of the donation ones! And they ran out here, but now I can't see them!"

"CREEPS!" shouted Harriet, hoping they could hear her.

"OI! YOU KIDS THERE! STOP!"

"Oh no! Security guard!" warned Harriet as we switched directions and began to run away from him too.

"Here! Take this!" I cried out to Harriet as I pushed the trolley with Ashley in it over to her.

I jumped up onto the nearest trolley park fence and tried to spot the thieves one last time.

"OVER THERE!" I shouted, pointing at a white van parked in the back corner of the car park. "QUICK!"

I set off towards the van, running so fast that I couldn't feel my legs any more. I could hear Ashley beginning to cry, but I couldn't stop. Just as I reached the van, the man and woman jumped into their seats and slammed the doors shut. We were too late!

"NOT SO FAST!" screamed Harriet as she and Ashley and their trolley reached me. She ripped open her rucksack, grabbed one of the tubs of slime and began throwing handfuls of it at the van just as fast as she could. In a few seconds, green splodges of oozy slime began to dribble and drool off the van windows and doors.

The van jumped forwards with a growl, making us all jump back a step.

"TAKE – THIS – ROBBERS!" panted Krish. He pushed his hands into his back pockets and pulled out the steaks. Pulling open the packet with a large "EUGH!", he threw the meat towards the van's windscreen.

We watched as the two big red steaks flew through the air and landed with loud thuds on the van's big front window.

"HA HA! Got you!" shouted Krish as a shower of crisps and chocolate splatted onto the van windows and stuck to the slime. Harriet and I had taken everything we had in our rucksacks and were throwing them at the van just as fast as we could.

"This is fun!" giggled Ashley as she threw crisps and hungrily stuck some into her mouth too. I wished we could have taken all the treats home instead, but we had to stop the thieves!

"GET OUT OF THE WAY, KIDS! BEFORE I REALLY HURT YA!" shouted the man in the van as he rolled down his window and stuck his head out, before making the van roar again.

When we didn't move, the man switched the headlights on and shook his fist at us.

"You better move!" screamed the woman, rolling her window down too. "He doesn't like kids who damage his van!"

"Yeah! Well, WE don't like thieves who steal our food!" I shouted.

Harriet pushed the trolley with Ashley in it out of the way, and Krish ran off to the side as the van roared again and jumped forwards.

But I didn't move.

The van roared again and again, and flashed its headlights at me like a giant monster.

But still I didn't move. Even though now I was getting scared.

The man behind the wheel was getting redder and angrier with every second.

"Nelson! Get out of the way!" shouted Krish as Ashley began to cry.

"NO!" I shouted back. "They're thieves! They're making other people go hungry! I won't move!"

From all around us, more and more people were beginning to stop to watch and listen. That was good, so I carried on shouting.

"THEY'RE FOOD BANK THIEVES! THEY
SWITCHED THEIR TROLLEY AND TOOK THE
DONATION TROLLEY!"

Inside the van, the man began to look
around as if now he was the one getting scared.
And the woman had put her head in her hands
as if she wanted to hide.

"That's awful!" I heard someone say.

"That's shocking!" cried a lady. "Someone
call the police!"

"Why's that van covered with slime and
meat, Daddy?" someone else asked.

The van growled and roared again as the
man inside shouted, "GET OUT OF MY WAY, KID!
OR I'LL RUN YOU DOWN!"

A long, loud beep made me take a step back.
But then someone suddenly stepped out in front
of me.

It was an old man.

And a few seconds later, a younger woman joined him.

And then three men. And then Krish and another kid I didn't know.

They were all coming to stand in front of me so that the van man couldn't hurt me!

"Exit the van with your hands up, NOW!" shouted a big man. It was the security guard that had been chasing after me and Ashley and Harriet and Krish just minutes before. He was sweating so much he looked as if he had just been for a swim.

"Come on! OUT! The jig is up!"

CHAPTER 9

The Equaliser

After the security guard shouted out those words of warning, people came running from all directions. The supermarket manager and lots of supermarket workers wearing bright orange vests came running up to the van and shouted at the thieves to open the doors. And then suddenly there were blue lights flashing and lots of police arrived too! All of them stood around the van as, at last, the man and woman gave up and came out with their hands in the air.

A police officer took their keys from them and opened up the back doors of the van.

Everyone gasped at the mountains of food stacked from the floor of the van to its roof.

"Whoah!" cried out Krish. "There must be fifty trolley loads in there! They're PROPER thieves!"

"That's about right," said the supermarket manager as she turned to look down at me and Harriet and Ashley and Krish. We stood in front of her, our hands all messy with bits of crisps and chocolate and blobs of slime.

"And you all helped stop them," the supermarket manager went on, her bright orange badge glinting down at us It told us her name was Onioke Samuels. "Thank you!"

"Well done, kids," shouted the old man who had stood in front of me to protect me from the van. He walked up and gave me a pat on the back. "You were so brave! They would have driven away if it weren't for you!"

From somewhere at the back of the crowd, someone cried out, "Heroes! Those kids are heroes!" and began to clap loudly.

And before we knew what was happening, it seemed everyone in the whole car park was clapping and shouting "HEROES!" at us too.

Ashley jumped up and down inside the trolley excitedly as Krish turned bright red. Harriet waved at everyone like a queen and took off her hat to give them a bow.

"Kids, come with me, please," said a police officer as he began to steer me through the crowd and back towards the supermarket. "We've got some questions to ask you all."

For the rest of the morning, the police and the supermarket manager and then all our parents asked us what felt like a thousand questions.

At first Harriet's mum and then Krish's mum and dad and then my mum were furious that we had sneaked out of Harriet's house in secret. They had already been worried because Harriet's sister had found us missing, and when they were called by the police, they had felt sick.

They all said they were going to ground us for the rest of our lives. But when they found out we had wanted to catch the thieves because everyone at Breakfast Club was starving, and that we had spent days and weeks spying on the trolleys and training and planning our stake-out, they all agreed that maybe they didn't need to ground us for that long after all.

Mum decided not to go back to work that day, and when we got home, she made me and Ashley two big cups of hot chocolate and asked us to tell her everything. Ashley pretended the trolley had turned into a rocket ship and that she had thrown millions of sweets at the thieves. But I told Mum the truth. And about how I never wanted the food bank to ever be empty again, and how I never wanted me or Lavinia or Kerry or anyone from Breakfast Club to have to have holes in their stomachs all the time.

Mum didn't say anything. But I knew she was thinking of lots of things she couldn't find the right words for.

*

The next day, everything went back to normal. It was a normal, boring Sunday, where I had to do homework and Ashley had to have the Sunday bath she always hated, and we all watched lots of telly.

But then on Monday morning, everything started to change.

First, a whole hour before I had to leave for school, the doorbell rang.

When Mum opened the door, a delivery man was standing in front of her with a giant basket of food tied with the most giant orange ribbon she had ever seen.

The basket was filled with every kind of food you could ever imagine – biscuits and popcorn and crisps and sweets and fruits and cheeses and breads and bananas and ... chocolate muffins!

"Who's it from?" I asked when Mum had screamed and made me and Ashley wake up and run to the front door too.

"Santa!" cried out Ashley.

But Mum shook her head. There was a small card tied to the basket, which Mum opened and showed me. "Read it, Nelson ..."

Inside the card, in scratchy writing, were the words:

Dear Nelson and Ashley,

Thank you for catching the trolley thieves! We and all the food banks we support are eternally grateful.

Love from everyone at Gladstores XXX

"And here," said the delivery man, smiling as he pulled something else from his back pocket and held it out to me. "This is for you too."

He handed me a folded-up newspaper.

I opened it – and gasped. There on the front page, above a huge picture of Noah Equiano, the best footballer in the world, was a giant headline that read:

SUPERMARKET TROLLEY GANG BUSTED IN FOOD BANK HEIST!

NOAH EQUIANO TAKES ACTION AFTER CHILDREN STOP DONATION THIEVES

I stared at Mum. She stared back and then gave me a hug so big I thought I could hear my bones creak.

After the delivery man left and we all ate the best breakfast any of us could ever remember eating, Mum read the newspaper out loud to me and Ashley. It told us that the man and woman we stopped had been part of a huge gang who had filled three huge warehouses with food stolen from lots of different supermarkets. They had been swapping donation trolleys with emptier trolleys from supermarkets for months, and then selling the food they had bought to smaller shops.

"The game is now over for the food bank robbers. All twenty-three members of their shameless gang are being questioned by the police," finished Mum. "Food banks nationwide are safe again."

"Good!" I said, feeling my insides swell up with pride.

Putting the newspaper down, Mum reached out and hugged me and Ashley again.

"Oh! I am so proud of my two little heroes," Mum whispered, before telling us to get ready quickly for school. But before I left the kitchen table, I stared at Mum's face for just as long as I could. I had nearly forgotten what it felt like to see Mum smiling her real smile. And I didn't ever want to forget it.

Then, at school, things got even better.

In Assembly, the Breakfast Club and everyone else gave me and Harriet and Krish and even Ashley a huge round of applause, and Mrs Bell called us up onto the stage to get some special certificates for bravery and determination!

And then something happened that was so amazing and so spectacular that I thought I had to be dreaming.

Because it wasn't Mrs Bell who gave us our certificates. Instead, she told the school that a very special guest wanted to do that and pointed to the back of the hall.

Mr Ramjit and Maureen the dinner lady gave everyone a wave and threw open the hall doors.

And there he was!

Noah Equiano – the REAL Noah Equiano!

The school burst into cheers as everyone got to their feet, and Krish screamed, "NO WAAAAAAAAAAAAAAAAAAAAAY!"

The real Noah Equiano came jogging up to the stage, waving at everyone and making Harriet hiccup so badly she had to clamp her hands over her mouth to make it stop.

It turned out that Noah Equiano hadn't come to our school just to give me and Krish and Harriet and Ashley a certificate. He had

come to tell us that he had been a member of
the Breakfast Club and the Free School Meals
Club too. And that because we had been so
brave and had helped hundreds of food banks
by stopping the thieves, he wanted to invite us

to Parliament so that we could help every child in the country get the food they needed to keep them strong and healthy and have an equal chance to do all the things they wanted to do – not just at school but after they finished school too.

And after Harriet stopped hiccupping, and Krish stopped silently screaming, and I could speak again, we all shouted, "YES!!"

Because who would say no to going on an adventure with The Equaliser to make sure that no one like me, or Ashley, or anyone at the Breakfast Club ever went to bed hungry again? Not anyone I can think of.

Except for, maybe, a thief.

Acknowledgements

This story only came into existence because of Marcus Rashford's tireless work to highlight the issue of food poverty and tackle those responsible. Marcus, you are a hero of our times: thank you for being the voice too many children have needed for far too long.

We are incredibly lucky to not only have heroes like Marcus Rashford but also s/heroes like Dame Emma Thompson and Jack Monroe righting wrongs and calling out government failures too. In addition, there is a hidden army of amazing hearts working in food banks and breakfast clubs every single day to help keep our little ones going. You are, each of you, stupendous.

I am deeply grateful to Ailsa Bathgate and the Barrington Stoke team for gifting me the space to create this story, and eternally thankful to the wondrous staff of Trussell Trust Food Banks, the Greggs Foundation Breakfast Club Programme, Sainsburys and Tesco for opening my eyes yet further as to what true and endless generosity looks like.

A percentage of all royalties earned from the sale of this book will be going towards Trussell Trust Food Banks, the Greggs Foundation Breakfast Club Programme and selected grassroots food bank charities. So to you, the wonderful reader of this story, thank you for helping Nelson's adventures and efforts go on.

What are food banks?

DID YOU KNOW? In the UK today, over 8 million people are struggling with food poverty. Just like Nelson and his family.

In the story, Nelson's mum works as a nurse, but at the end of some months she just doesn't have enough money to buy all the things that her family needs. So they have to visit a food bank for help.

Food banks provide emergency food to people who really need it. Thousands of very kind people donate to food banks at different places such as supermarkets, schools, churches, doctors' surgeries and some businesses too, every single day. And lots of supermarkets and local shops also donate millions of pounds' worth of food every year to help food banks too.

That's why food banks are incredibly special – they are made up entirely of gifts given by people wanting to help other people.

If you would like to learn more about food banks and how they help children like Nelson, have a look at **www.trusselltrust.org** or **www.fareshare.org.uk**.

Why do people need to use food banks?

That's a very good question!

The UK is a very wealthy country – the sixth richest country in the world according to some measurements. And we live in a country where there is lots of food. So much in fact that 6.7 million tonnes of food (that's over £10 billion worth of food!) goes to waste in the UK every year! But the rate of food poverty in the UK is among the highest in Europe.

So why are so many people struggling?

Food poverty is part of a much bigger problem. Millions of families in the UK are struggling to pay their rent or bills for water and fuel. They may be waiting for the government to act faster to help them; they may be unable to find a well-paid job or, like Nelson's mum, they might have a landlord who keeps increasing their rent and, as a result, they may be in debt. Because of problems like these, there is often not enough money to cover every cost, even when all the grown-ups in a home are working.

This is a situation that can happen to anyone, and people who need to use food banks should never feel ashamed because they need help. It's actually one of the bravest things in the world to do: to ask for help when you need it.

What are breakfast clubs?

As the name suggests, breakfast clubs are ... clubs which serve breakfast! Yum!

They often open an hour before school starts, and most are run in schools and overseen by lovely teachers, teaching assistants, catering staff and volunteers.

As you may have heard, "breakfast is the most important meal of the day"! It is, after all, the meal that breaks your night's fast (hence the name) and gives your body the energy it needs to get going for the day ahead.

But for many of us, breakfast becomes a missed meal – usually because everyone is in a rush to get out of the door! For many parents/guardians who work, there simply isn't time to get breakfast ready for everyone. And for those who are having a tough week and struggling with food poverty, there may not be enough food in the house to provide a nutritious breakfast.

That's why breakfast clubs are probably one of the best kinds of clubs around. They help parents/guardians stop worrying, *and* they give everyone a chance to start the day with a full tummy. If you would like to learn more about breakfast clubs, or if your school would like help setting one up, have a look at **www.greggsfoundation.org.uk/breakfast-clubs**.

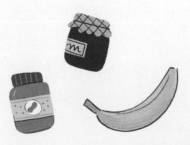

Three ways you can help food banks and breakfast clubs

DID YOU KNOW? While food banks may have "food" in the title, they don't just give things to eat and drink to the people they help. They also give other essential items like toiletries, tampons, nappies and baby food too. And lots of breakfast clubs don't only provide breakfast, they provide games, space and tools for children and young people to do their homework before school starts.

Here are three ways you can help your local food banks and your school too:

1. Find out what they need

In order to give people what they need, it's better to ask and know for sure rather than make a guess. This also stops the creation of extra food waste.

For food banks: check out the Trussell Trust website and type in your postcode. This will help you find your nearest food bank as well as learn all about what food and non-food donations they need.

For breakfast clubs: ask your head teacher if there is anything that is needed (games, books, maybe even computers) that you can donate or help raise funds for.

2. Help tackle "Holiday Hunger"

During the school holidays when there are no free school meals and fewer breakfast clubs available, many families find it even more difficult to access the food they need. Lots of businesses, charities and faith groups (from cafes and supermarkets to community centres, churches, mosques and temples) work even harder at these times to raise donations and distribute help to local families. There is now a map of lots of these organisations at **www.endchildfoodpoverty.org/help**. Use it to find any help you may need, or to find out how you can help them in their work.

3. Join the #EndChildFoodPoverty campaign at www.endchildfoodpoverty.org!

On this site, you will find the latest actions being taken to encourage the UK government to help end food poverty, as well as lots of facts and tips on how to help too.

Our books are tested
for children and young people by
children and young people.

Thanks to everyone who consulted on
a manuscript for their time and effort in
helping us to make our books better
for our readers.

sy, Es

...thor of *The Survival of the Habsburg Empire.*
...itor of *Europe's Balance of Power, 1815–1848*, and has written articles on British and Habsburg history in both English and German. He is currently writing another book on the Habsburg Monarchy, as well as a history of Europe in the nineteenth century. He reviews for *The Times Literary Supplement* and for several learned journals.

Chris Cook was educated at St Catharine's College, Cambridge, and Nuffield College, Oxford, and is currently Head of the Department of History, Philosophy and Contemporary European Studies at the Polytechnic of North London. He has previously been Lecturer in Politics at Magdalen College, Oxford, and Senior Research Officer at the London School of Economics. His previous publications include the six volume *Sources in British Political History* and (with co-authors) *The Slump, By-Elections in British Politics* and *The Politics of Reappraisal*. A Fellow of the Royal Historical Society, he is also Editor of *Pears Cyclopaedia* and co-author of the *Guardian* General Election Guides.